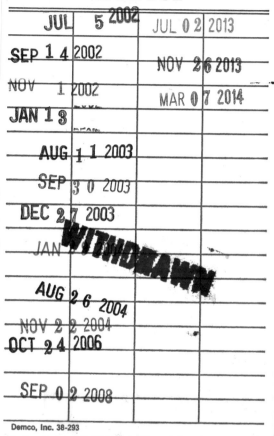

A Boy Named Charlie Brown

A Boy Named Charlie Brown

Charles M. Schulz

MetroBooks

Copyright © 1969 by United Feature Syndicate, Inc.

Based on the Lee Mendelson-Bill Melendez feature film,
A Boy Named Charlie Brown, screenplay by Charles M. Schulz.

This edition is reprinted by MetroBooks,
by arrangement with Henry Holt and Company, LLC.

2001 MetroBooks

ISBN 1-58663-188-8

Printed and bound in the United States of America

01 02 03 04 05 MC 9 8 7 6 5 4 3 2 1

RRD

To Barbara, Helen and Joyce from
Lee, Bill and Sparky

The last time Charlie Brown's team won a ball game, he was home sick in bed. Losing all the games was bad enough, but the thing that bothered him the most was that he knew the games really weren't very important. They meant a lot to him, but no one else seemed to care. If you lose an important ball game, and if a lot of people care, then it's different. But when you are playing ball games that no one knows anything about, somehow losing seems even more terrible.

Sometimes the appearance of the field itself was very aggravating to Charlie Brown. On one particular day, he walked out to the field feeling in just the right mood to play a great ball game.

But what did he see? His pitcher's mound was covered with dandelions. Now, no self-respecting pitcher can ever be expected to pitch a good game from a mound that is covered with dandelions.

And then he got into an argument with Schroeder, his catcher, over signals. Schroeder said to him, "One finger will mean the high straight ball and two fingers will mean the low straight ball."

"What about my curve?" asked Charlie Brown.
"And my slider and my knuckle ball? And what about
my drop? You forgot about my famous drop ball."

"One finger will mean the high straight ball," said
Schroeder, "and two fingers will mean the low straight
ball."

On the very first pitch of the game, Charlie Brown was hit on the head with a line drive.

While he was lying on the mound feeling kind of dizzy, all the kids clustered about him and Linus asked, "Does anyone here know anything about first aid?"

Lucy, in her usual straightforward way, said, "It's probably not serious... second or third aid will do."

Poor Charlie Brown heard this, and cried out, "I'm dying and all I hear are insults!"

Later in the day when Charlie Brown was feeling completely depressed, Linus tried to explain to him that he really shouldn't regard himself as a loser. "I don't believe that some people are born losers, Charlie Brown. I think this is all foolishness. I think that if you try hard enough and long enough, you can be just as good at something as anyone else."

While they were talking, the two boys sketched a tic-tac-toe diagram in the sand in front of them and began to fill in the squares with X's and O's.

Linus said, "Don't give up, Charlie Brown. You're a good ball player, and if you keep trying you're going to win your share of ball games. You are *not* a born loser! You can learn to win at things just as much as anyone else!"

Just as Linus said this, he drew a line from one corner of the tic-tac-toe diagram to the other and suddenly realized he had beaten Charlie Brown.

The next morning, the two boys were walking to school and they met some of the girls who were discussing a spelling bee that was to take place that day.

"Why don't you enter the spelling bee, Charlie Brown?" asked Linus. "I'll bet if you won something like that it would do great things for your morale."

All the girls started to laugh and ridicule Linus's suggestion, and they told Charlie Brown that if he didn't want to make a fool out of himself, he should forget the idea right away.

When they got to school, however, Charlie Brown decided that he would raise his hand and volunteer for the spelling bee, but as he got his hand halfway up it stopped.

"My hand won't go up," Charlie Brown said. "My hand is smarter than I am."

But then his hand did go up and the teacher was quite sur-
prised because Charlie Brown was not one who volunteered for a
lot of things. Most of the time he was kind of shy. This time, however, he went up to the front of the class and joined the others. And,
strangely enough, things went right for him. Each word that he
was given was all too familiar.

"Of course Charlie Brown knows how to spell 'failure,'" said Lucy when he was given his first word. "He's been a failure all his life."

Before he knew it, Charlie Brown had beaten all of the other kids in the class, and had won the spelling bee.

On the way home from school, Linus congratulated Charlie Brown and said, "If you want me to, I'll help you study for the next round."

They dug out all sorts of dictionaries and books with lots of spelling rules in them, and Charlie Brown began to memorize as many of the rules as he could.

As the afternoon wore on, Linus and Charlie Brown found that it was fun. And when Snoopy joined them with his Snoopy Harp, they even danced around the room and sang a little song about "I Before E Except After C."

The next day, however, Charlie Brown's head was filled with a jumble of rules.

I before E

When he stood in front of the whole school with the rest of the contestants, he was sure he was going to faint.

"He doesn't have a chance," Lucy said to Violet. "He's up against some of the best spellers in the school."

Everything went smoothly for Charlie Brown until the last word "perceive" was given to him.

"He's doomed," moaned Lucy. "He'll never get that word."

The only thing that saved Charlie Brown was the little tune that Snoopy began to play on his harp as he sat outside the school window.

"I Before E Except After C," said the song, and suddenly Charlie Brown remembered.

"Perceive," Charlie Brown said. "P-E-R-C-E-I-V-E.
Perceive."

He had won!

You have never heard so much shrieking and yelling in all your life. Kids were jumping up and down and turning around...

...and they even carried Charlie Brown home on their shoulders like he was a real hero.

That afternoon, everyone gathered at Charlie Brown's house to congratulate him upon his remarkable victory. All Charlie Brown could say was, "Whew! I'm glad that's over. It was great to win, but it sure was a nerve-racking experience."

"What do you mean over?" cried Lucy. "This is just the beginning. Now you have to go to New York and be in the national finals. You can't quit now. You can't let your class and your school down. You have to represent us all!"

"National finals!"

"AUGH!"

A few days later, all the kids said good-bye to Charlie Brown and put him on the special chartered bus that was to take him to the big city.

Linus handed Charlie Brown his blanket and said, "Here, take this for good luck."

"I can't take your blanket, Linus. This is your security blanket. You will need it."

"Take it," said Linus. "Take it. I want you to have it. Take it!"

"I feel like I'm being drafted," said Charlie Brown.

The next thing Charlie Brown knew, the bus was pulling down
the street and he was on his way to the national finals.

It was a lonely ride, but when they finally reached New York, Charlie Brown and his fellow contestants got off the bus and stood on the sidewalk looking up at the city's tall skyscrapers.

Then the teacher in charge took them to their hotel near the auditorium where the contestants would gather the next day for the finals. The boys and girls found their hotel rooms and after putting away their things they opened their books and began to study.

Not long after Charlie Brown's bus left, Linus knew he had made a mistake. He began to feel dizzy and he discovered that it was hard for him to breathe. He hadn't realized how much he depended upon his blanket to keep him going from day to day. He felt like he was going to fall over at any minute, and he knew if he didn't get his blanket back quickly he would become seriously ill.

There was another bus leaving soon, so Linus asked Snoopy if he would go with him to try to find Charlie Brown and get his blanket back.

Whenever Snoopy traveled, he always carried his dog dish with him because he knew how difficult it was to find good dog dishes when you are in a strange neighborhood.

They made a pecu-
liar-looking pair. Linus
looked very distraught
and his eyes had a glazed
appearance. He needed
that blanket. Snoopy, of
course, was very relaxed
because none of this
really meant very much
to him. He was willing
to go along for the ride,
but he really never paid
much attention to what
the kids in the neighbor-
hood were doing because
he always had more im-
portant things on his
mind. This is the way it
is when you are a dog.

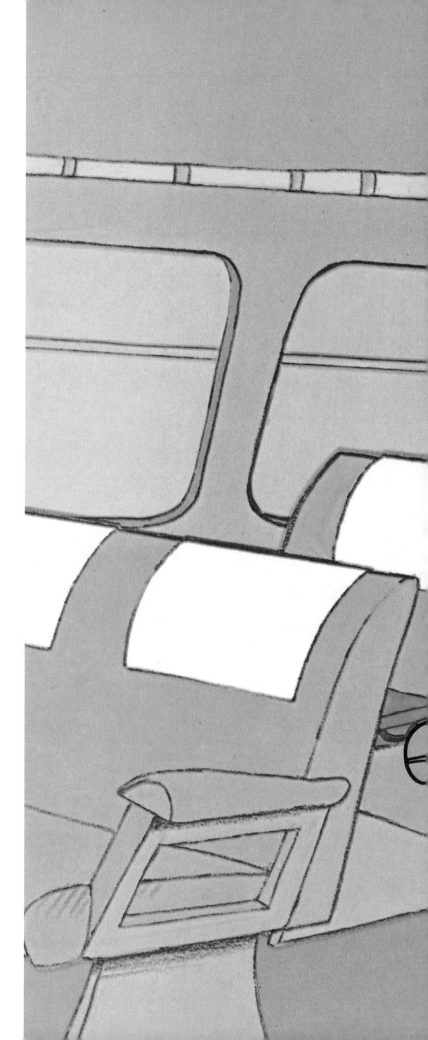

After studying in his room for several hours Charlie Brown began to get hungry. He decided to call room service and order a sandwich and a glass of milk.

When Charlie Brown heard a knock on the door, he thought it was the bell-boy. But instead it turned out to be Snoopy and Linus. When Snoopy and Charlie Brown saw each other they danced around in delight.

But the first thing that Linus wanted to know was, "Where's my blanket?"

"I don't know where your blanket is, Linus," Charlie Brown said. "I've been so busy studying and worrying about tomorrow that I just haven't paid any attention. I think I've misplaced it. Maybe it is down in the hotel lobby or out on the sidewalk someplace."

"Out on the sidewalk!" shrieked Linus. "Good grief! I gave you my blanket for good luck and you *think* you left it out on the sidewalk! How could you do this to me?"

"I'm sorry, Linus," Charlie Brown said. "I've just too many other things to think about."

"Out on the sidewalk!" shrieked Linus again. "I can't stand it!"

"Why don't you take Snoopy and walk around?" suggested Charlie Brown. "Maybe you will be able to find it. Snoopy is a good hunting dog."

Linus and Snoopy went out the door, down the elevator, and onto the street.

Snoopy and Linus looked all over but they could not find the blanket. They looked behind trash cans, mailboxes, and everything else that looked like it might be hiding a security blanket. Linus was really depressed because he knew there was little chance of finding his blanket in the streets of a big city like this.

Snoopy helped Linus for a while, but then he forgot what they were looking for when they came across a beautiful outdoor skating rink.

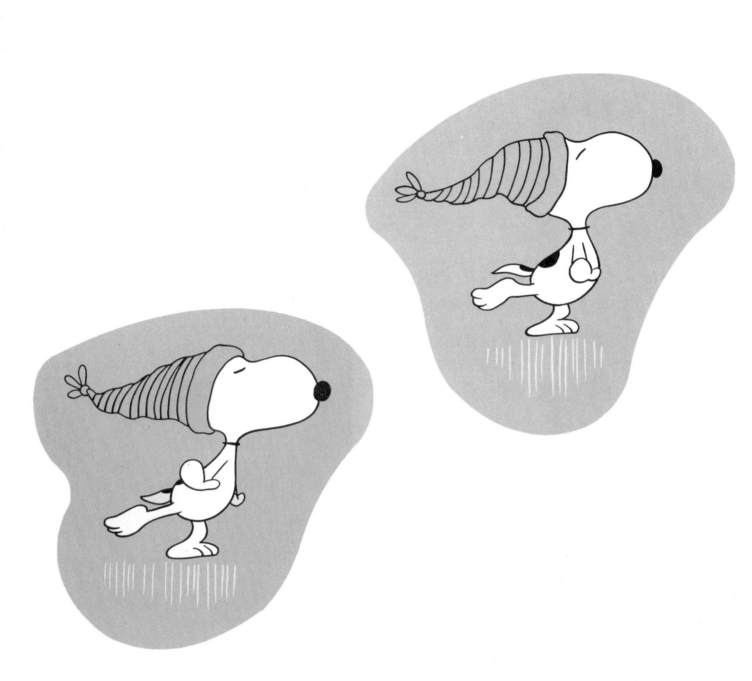

Snoopy pretended he was a world famous figure-skater and
he went through a beautiful four-minute routine.

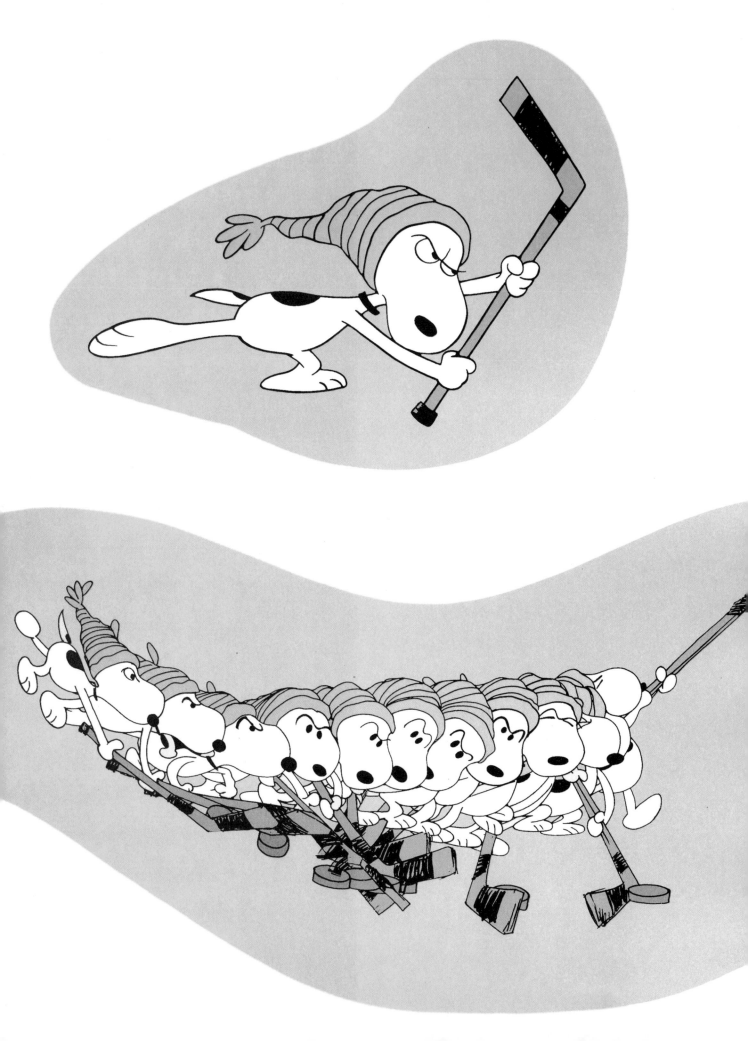

He also pretended he was a great hockey player and that he had just scored the winning goal in the final game of the Stanley Cup playoffs.

Linus was furious with Snoopy when he discovered that this so-called hunting dog was no help at all.

When they got back to the hotel, Linus was so mad he could hardly talk.

"You and your stupid dog, Charlie Brown," he said. "You make me so mad! He is no help at all. He couldn't find *anything!* And as for you . . . I'll never loan you my blanket again!"

"I'm sorry, I really am," said Charlie Brown. "And I'd like to help you find your blanket because I know it was my fault that your blanket was lost. But I have got to get ready for the contest. I must get dressed and shine my shoes."

As Charlie Brown said this he reached beneath his bed and pulled out a rag to dust off his shoes.

"My blanket!" cried Linus. "You're shining your shoes with my blanket!" And, sure enough, there was Linus's security blanket that everyone thought had been lost forever.

Now the three friends were able to set off for the national spelling bee finals.

As they neared the auditorium they could see all sorts of people flowing into the huge building. And, of course, Charlie Brown began to get very nervous.

"Good luck, Charlie Brown," said Linus. "Snoopy and I will be sitting in the first row watching you."

After Linus and Snoopy wished Charlie Brown good luck, they walked through the main lobby and down the long aisle to their seats by the stage.

Charlie Brown's friends had gathered around a television set to watch the contest.

When the spelling bee started, Charlie Brown managed to get through the first rounds, but a few of the other entrants weren't so lucky.

"Irritable," said one girl. "I-R-R-I-T-I-B-L-E. Irritable."

"Recommend," said a boy. "R-E-C-O-M-E-N-D. Recommend."

Before Charlie Brown knew it there was only one person standing between him and the championship.

Charlie Brown's next word was fussbudget. "Fussbudget," Charlie Brown said confidently. "F-U-S-S-B-U-D-G-E-T. Fussbudget."

Back home Lucy said, "Hey, how did he know that word?"

Charlie Brown's opponent spelled his next word correctly and then it was Charlie Brown's turn again.

When his word was given, Charlie Brown said, "'Beagle'? the word is 'beagle'?"

The kids leaned forward in anticipation.

At the theater Snoopy began to leap up and down
and wave his paws.

"Beagle," said Charlie Brown. "B-E-A-G-E-L. Beagle."

"AUGH!"

"AUGH!"

"AUGH!"

"That blockhead!" cried Lucy. "He couldn't even spell the brand of his own dog."

Charlie Brown was crushed. He sat in his chair on the stage as everyone congratulated the student who had won first place. Then, after everyone had left the auditorium, he walked up the aisle with his head down.

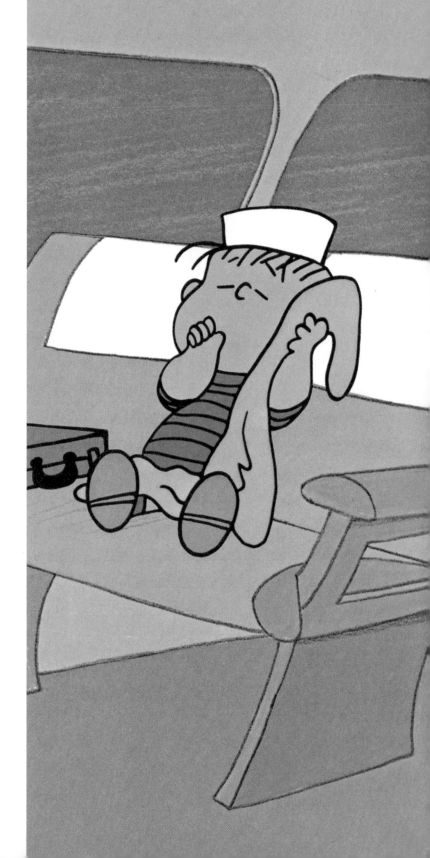

All the way home on the bus that night Charlie Brown could think of only one thing. He was the goat again. He could have been the hero, but he was the goat. He had let down all his friends who had believed in him. Why couldn't he ever do anything right?

When they reached their home town, Linus, Charlie Brown, and Snoopy gathered up their belongings and climbed down the steps of the bus. Linus looked around and said, "I guess nobody realized we were returning."

Charlie Brown was so depressed he couldn't even answer when Linus said good-night to him.

He just walked slowly home and crawled into bed and lay there in the dark feeling sorry for himself.

The next day Linus stopped by Charlie Brown's house after school and knocked on the door. Charlie Brown's little sister, Sally, answered the door, and when he asked her where Charlie Brown was she said, "He's in his room. He didn't go to school today. He just lies there in bed in the dark with all the shades pulled down."

Linus went upstairs and tapped on the bedroom door and then opened it slowly.

"May I come in Charlie Brown?" he said.

"What are you doing?" asked Charlie Brown.

"I just want to raise the shade," answered Linus as he tiptoed into the room and went over to one of the windows. "I just stopped by to see how you are."

"I don't want to talk to anybody."

"But I have good news," said Linus. "Our team won a ball game today."

"Oh, great."

"Everyone missed you," continued Linus. "It was a pretty good game." Then he paused for a moment and said, "Aren't you going to get up, Charlie Brown?"

"No," said Charlie Brown. "I'm just going to lie here for the rest of my life."

"Well, I think I know how you feel," said Linus. "It was kind of hard on you losing that spelling bee because I know you really tried, and I know how hard you studied, and I know that you feel you let everyone down." Linus went over to the door, and then turned around and said, "But did you notice something, Charlie Brown?"

"What's that?"

"The world didn't come to an end," said Linus, and he walked out of the room and closed the door.

Charlie Brown looked up at the ceiling for a while and then finally sat up in bed. He reached down and put on one sock, and then the other, and then he slipped on his shirt with the jagged stripes that he always wore.

When he went outside he noticed that everything
in the neighborhood seemed to be pretty much the same.

Some of the girls were jumping rope...

...and a group of boys were shooting marbles.

And then, suddenly, way off in the distance, he saw Lucy kneeling in the grass with a football. She was just lazily tossing it back and forth in her hand, and every now and then she would hold it out in front of her as if she were expecting someone to come along for the kickoff.

Charlie Brown recalled the number of times that Lucy had tricked him by promising to hold the ball while he came running up to kick it. Without fail she would jerk the football away at the last moment and he would fly through the air and land on his back.

A look of fierce determination came to Charlie Brown, and a little smile grew on his face. This time he was going to surprise her. He hid for a moment behind a large tree and then suddenly leaped to his feet and ran across the yard furiously.

He made a wild kick at the football which Lucy
had propped up in front of her.

But just before his foot made contact with the ball,
she pulled it away and Charlie Brown landed flat on
his back.

Lucy leaned over Charlie Brown and said, "Welcome home, Charlie Brown."